Catch!

Ball

Drum

I like banging
on a drum.

Bang! bang!

Oh no! Am I
making lots
of noise?

Hello!

Mmm ... this
rattle is tasty.

Do you
want a go?

Rattle

Say "hello", Teddy.

Would you like
a big red bow?

Teddy bear

But where's everyone else, Teddy?

I'm off on my
tricycle–
see you later!

Tricycle

Catch me if
you can!

Do these rings
go here?

Or here?

Coloured rings

Maybe I'll play with my building blocks instead.

Quack!
Quack!

These ducks
are going
swimming.
Off they go!

Duck

Close your eyes
for a surprise.

It's a present!

What's inside?

Present

This edition published by Lorenz Books in 2001

© Anness Publishing Limited 1996, 2001

Lorenz Books is an imprint of
Anness Publishing Limited
Hermes House
88–89 Blackfriars Road
London SE1 8HA

www.lorenzbooks.com

This edition distributed in Canada by
Raincoast Books
9050 Shaughnessy Street, Vancouver,
British Columbia V6P 6E5

10 9 8 7 6 5 4 3 2 1

Publisher: Joanna Lorenz
Managing Editor, Children's Books:
	Gilly Cameron Cooper
Senior Editor/Text: Caroline Beattie
Editorial Assistant: Rosalind Anderson
Photographer: Lucy Tizard
Design and Typesetting: Michael Leaman
	Design Partnership
Production Controller: Joanna King

The Publishers would like to thank the
following children (and their parents) for
appearing in this book: Daisy May
Bryant, April Cain, Jamie Grant, Thomas
Grant, Magdalena Nawrocka-Weekes,
Ella Wilks-Harper, Jordan Woods.

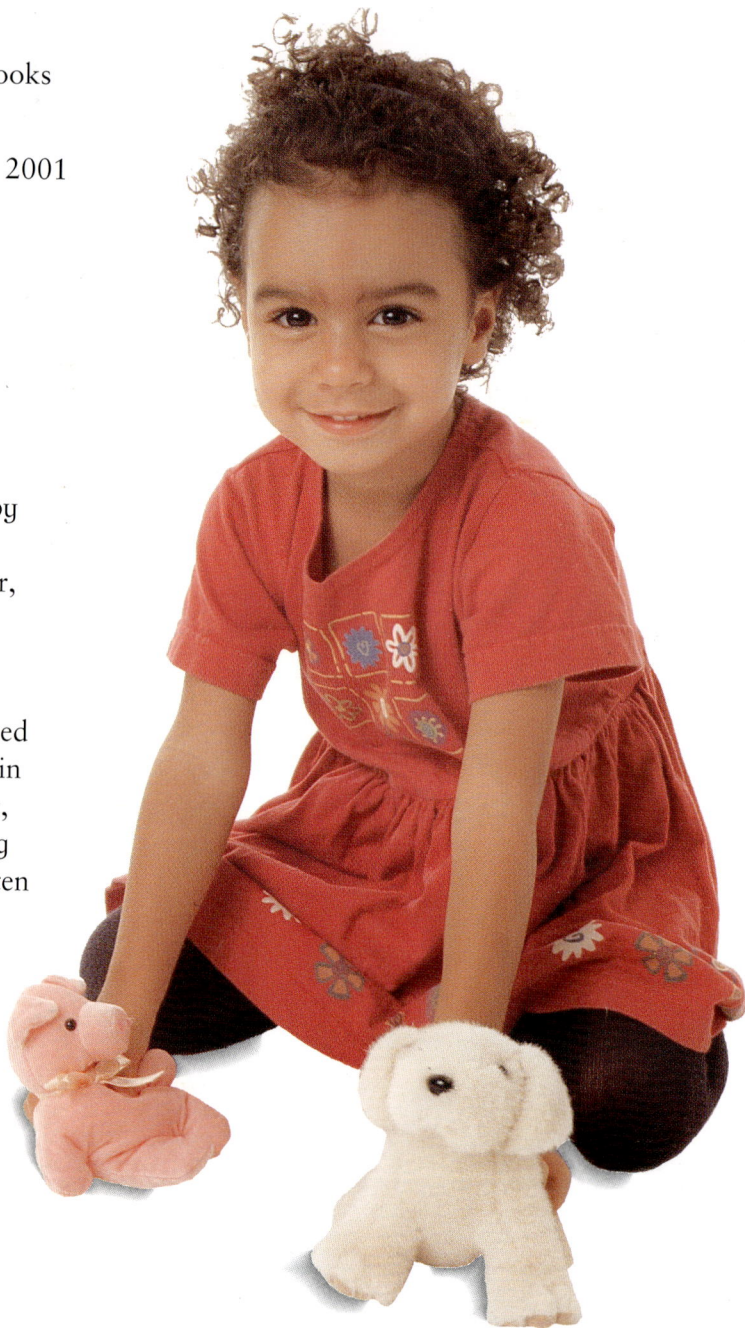